Bantam Books in the Choose Your Own Adventure® series
Ask your bookseller for the books you have missed

THE LUCKIEST DAY OF YOUR LIFE

BY EDWARD PACKARD

ILLUSTRATED BY TOM LA PADULA

BANTAM BOOKS

NEW YORK • TORONTO • LONDON • SYDNEY • AUCKLAND

RL 4, age 10 and up

THE LUCKIEST DAY OF YOUR LIFE
A Bantam Book / February 1993

CHOOSE YOUR OWN ADVENTURE® is a registered trademark of Bantam Books, a division of Bantam Doubleday Dell Publishing Group, Inc. Registered in U.S. Patent and Trademark Office and elsewhere.

Original conception of Edward Packard

Cover art by Daniel Horne
Interior illustrations by Tom La Padula

ISBN 0-553-29304-4

Published simultaneously in the United States and Canada

Bantam Books are published by Bantam Books, a division of Bantam Doubleday Dell Publishing Group, Inc. Its trademark, consisting of the words "Bantam Books" and the portrayal of a rooster, is Registered in U.S. Patent and Trademark Office and in other countries. Marca Registrada. Bantam Books, 666 Fifth Avenue, New York, New York 10103.

PRINTED IN THE UNITED STATES OF AMERICA

OPM   0 9 8 7 6 5 4 3 2 1

THE LUCKIEST DAY OF YOUR LIFE

WARNING!!!

Do not read this book straight through from beginning to end. These pages contain many different adventures that you may have when you receive a mysterious good-luck charm at a traveling carnival.

From time to time as you read along, you'll have a chance to make a choice. After you make your decision, follow the instructions to find out what happens to you next.

A lucky charm won't be much help if you make foolish choices, so think carefully before you act. If you keep your wits about you, you're in for the luckiest day of your life!

Good luck!

It's a hot July evening. You and your friends, Luke and Liz Stedman, are at a traveling carnival that has come to your town. You've already been on most of the rides, and now you're just strolling around, looking at the game booths and sideshows. You notice a booth with a sign over it that reads

**TAKE A CHANCE AND WIN A RIDE
IN A HOT-AIR BALLOON
VALUE $100
ONLY 25 CENTS A TICKET
GET A BIRD'S-EYE VIEW OF THE WORLD
THRILL TO THIS ONCE-IN-A-LIFETIME
ADVENTURE!**

"My cousin went on one of those balloon rides once," you say. "He said it was great."

"Let's each buy a ticket," Liz says.

The three of you pay your quarters, and the attendant gives you your tickets. You stuff yours in your pocket.

A few minutes later, you stop before a ball-toss booth. It has a white wall in the back with a circular hole in it. A basket of colored plastic balls sits on the counter in front. A sign over the booth says,

**TOSS THE BALL THROUGH THE HOLE
AND WIN A GREAT PRIZE
—50 CENTS A TOSS—**

Turn to page 2.

2

"It looks impossible," Luke says. "The hole is hardly any bigger than the balls."

"The prizes had better be good," you say. "This looks like an easy way to lose fifty cents."

A man with a long, pointed beard is tending the booth. He points toward a shelf with some inexpensive-looking prizes arranged on it. "Get the ball through the hole and you can have a prize greater than you could ever imagine," he says.

You and your friends exchange glances. You know they must be thinking the same thing you are—this looks like a real scam.

"I think it's too hard," Luke says. "I'm not going to play."

"What do you mean by 'prize greater than we could ever imagine'?" you ask the man.

His blue eyes glitter as he looks at you. "You'll find out if you win."

"I'll give it a try," Liz says with a shrug. She gives the attendant two quarters, and he hands her a ball. Liz aims carefully and tosses it, but it hits the rim of the hole and bounces off. "There goes fifty cents," she says.

Go on to the next page.

You know getting the ball through the hole is a long shot, but you can't help being curious about the prize. You drop fifty cents on the counter, pick up a ball, and squint at the target. You can see that the ball will have to be going straight to make it through the hole. It can't come at an angle. You'll have to throw it fast. You wind up like a baseball pitcher and let the ball fly.

It whizzes through the hole. What a lucky throw!

Go on to the next page.

4

Luke and Liz cheer and slap you on the back. The attendant looks amazed. He shakes his head. "I never thought anyone would do it."

"Well, you thought wrong," you say with a grin. "Now it's time for a prize greater than any I could ever imagine."

"I have two great prizes for you to choose from," the man says. He takes a couple of small objects off the shelf and puts them on the counter in front of you. One is a greenish-blue crystal about the size of a cherry. It glistens in the light and seems quite unusual, but it certainly doesn't look valuable. The other prize is a tiny book, so thin that there can't be more than a few pages in it. The title of the book is *How to Get Lucky*.

Luke is trying not to laugh. "Those are the prizes?" he says sarcastically.

"Greater than you could ever imagine?" says Liz in the same tone of voice.

Turn to page 60.

"Maybe she's a stretch runner," Louis says. But even as he's talking, Clementine is falling further behind.

Meanwhile, Caper has moved up fast and taken the lead at the half-mile post. Bright Star is second and Songfest third, while Palindrome has dropped back to fourth place.

You keep your eye on the leaders—you've practically given up hope on your horse. Then Louis elbows you and starts to yell. You look where he's pointing and see that Clementine is coming up fast on the outside. She passes two horses as if they were standing still. She's neck and neck with Songfest at the three-quarter-mile mark.

"Wow!" Louis yells, and you start yelling too as the leaders fade on the homestretch. Clementine, running hard, passes Caper just before the wire and wins by a nose!

Louis grins and claps you on the shoulder. "That crystal of yours really works. We're going to be rolling in dough soon!"

You grin back at him, but you're feeling a little uncomfortable. Even though you just picked one winner, you're not sure you believe the crystal was really responsible.

Louis is so excited that his hands are trembling. He holds the program in front of you. "Okay. What's your pick for the third race?"

Turn to page 32.

"I guess I'll take the crystal," you say. You pick up the shiny greenish-blue object and look at it more closely. It still doesn't look very special to you.

The attendant winks at you. "You're going to have very, very good luck from now on."

"If it's such a lucky thing to have, why are you giving it up?" you ask.

"It's only lucky for the right person," he says. "When you threw the ball through the hole it meant that you were the right person."

You toss the crystal in the air and catch it. "Well, we'll see if you're right," you say.

You and your friends continue to wander around the carnival grounds. You try a few more games, but you can't seem to win any more prizes.

The three of you stop at the snack stand for a soda before calling it quits for the night. Luke and Liz take turns examining the crystal.

"It will look neat sitting on your desk," Liz says.

"That's good," you say, "because it's been almost an hour since I won it and I haven't had a single bit of good luck yet."

Luke pats your shoulder. "Be patient. It may take a while to work."

Turn to page 79.

The next Saturday morning you wake up early, wolf down your breakfast, and rush out to your bike. Luke and Liz are waiting for you when you reach their house.

"I can't wait," says Liz. "This is going to be awesome!" You and Luke nod in agreement.

By the time you get to Bennett's Farm, the balloon has already been inflated. You can see it in an empty pasture as you bike up the road. It's tied down with ropes snagged around stakes in the ground. The balloon, with its blue and yellow stripes, is an eye-catching sight, swaying and tugging in the breeze. A small crowd is standing by to watch the launch.

You lean your bikes against the stump of an old maple and run over to the balloon. The balloonist shakes your hands. He's a gaunt-eyed, thin-faced man in his thirties.

"My name is Mistislav Schervenadski," he says. "But you can call me Micky." He introduces you to a rather elderly woman named Miss Johnstone who will be going on the ride with you. She looks a bit old to be going up in a balloon, you think, but you figure that's her business. Micky helps her up into the basket, and you and your friends climb aboard after her.

Turn to page 80.

Three weeks later, you, Luke, and Liz find yourselves in court, telling your story to the judge.

Fortunately, the three of you get off pretty easily. The judge sentences you to six months of community service. You'll have to sweep floors every Saturday at the Youth Center.

You're still trying to figure out how to get lucky.

The End

You grab the book back from Luke and wave it at the attendant. "I thought this was going to be a book on how to get lucky," you say. "First of all, it doesn't say anything about luck. Second of all, it's only got one page, and there's not much on that, either."

Luke leans over the counter and glares at the attendant. "This is a real scam. It ought to be against the law."

"It probably *is* against the law," Liz says.

The attendant takes the book and looks at the page. "No," he says. "This is what I thought it was. It's short, but that's all that's needed to tell you how to be lucky." He looks you in the eye. "Just getting this book makes this the luckiest day of your life."

"This is crazy," you say.

"We'll see what the manager has to say about this," Luke adds.

Turn to page 81.

12

Three weeks later you're standing on the brightly lit stage of *True? Or False?* The game is almost over, and so far you're doing very well. The studio audience stares up at you expectantly as the glitzy host of the show, Merv Becker, gives you a toothy smile. "Well," he says heartily, "you're doing great so far. You've already won over five thousand dollars, and you are the only contestant left in the game. Are you ready for the all-or-nothing final question?"

"I sure am, Merv," you say. You don't really feel very ready, but you were told before the show to act cheerful when you're on camera.

"Terrific. All right, then." Merv unfolds another slip of paper. "You'll have ten seconds to answer. If you know or guess the right answer, you get this week's Surprise Prize. If you admit you don't know, you get to keep your winnings so far of five thousand, three hundred dollars. If you guess the wrong answer, you lose everything."

Turn to page 22.

14

When you get home from the studio there's a message for you on the answering machine. It's from Luke and Liz. When you call them back, they get on separate lines so that all three of you can talk at once.

"Wow. We watched the show. You were great," Luke exclaims.

"You must have had your lucky crystal with you," Liz says.

"As a matter of fact, I did," you say. "Hey, you two were with me when I won the crystal. I think you should be the ones to come with me on the safari."

"I'd love to," they both say at once.

Turn to page 23.

You start to get up, then collapse back into your seat. Your legs feel as if they're not connected to your body. You try again and manage to get unsteadily to your feet. Liz helps support you. Then you notice she's holding one foot off the floor.

"Are you hurt?"

She nods. "I think it's sprained."

You take a deep breath. "Has Jake radioed for help? Do we know when we might get rescued?"

Liz shakes her head. "He can't. The radio's out."

Turn to page 35.

You continue to watch the sights passing by below as the balloon drifts along. A dog stands in the middle of a field, barking at you. A few minutes later you pass over some kids who have gotten off their bicycles to watch you go by.

"Hey look, there's Jen," Liz says. She leans over the rim of the basket to wave at her friend.

"Don't lean over the edge, dummy," Luke says, yanking her back.

"I wasn't leaning over the edge," Liz says.

At that moment you notice Miss Johnstone. She's huddled down on the floor of the basket, whimpering softly.

"You okay, Miss Johnstone?" you ask.

"No!" Her face wears a tortured expression. "I didn't think I'd be scared, but I'm terrified. I don't think I can stand it much longer. Take me down, please!"

Micky glances at her. "You'll be all right, Miss Johnstone. We'll be down in about forty minutes. You don't need to worry."

The old woman seems to shrivel up. "Please, please take me down!"

"It would be inconvenient to put down here. The van is picking us up at the airstrip," Micky says. "Besides, the town's just ahead. It's our big chance to see it from the air. It wouldn't be fair to the others to land so soon."

Turn to page 85.

18

Kwame laughs. "There are many strange things in Africa," he says. "But all our mountains are connected to the ground."

"We can't see the bottom because of the haze," Martha explains.

"Right," Kwame says, "but the air higher up is crystal clear."

"It must be cold, too," you say. "That looks like snow at the top."

"It sure is," says Kwame. "Even though Kilimanjaro is almost on the equator."

"It's so huge," Liz says. "It almost doesn't look real."

Kwame nods. "The Ngorongoro crater was once a gigantic mountain, too. But one day millions of years ago, it blew its top. Now it's the largest crater in the world. The huge plain within the crater is more or less isolated from the area around it, and there's a lake in the middle of it, so it has attracted a great number and variety of animals."

Your party spends the night at a lodge near the outer rim of the crater. The next morning you take the Land Rover up to the nine-thousand-foot-high rim. For most of the way the view is obstructed by trees. The road becomes progressively more rutted, and parts of it have been half washed away by heavy rains. Finally you reach a bluff overlooking the vast plain below. You stare down three thousand feet into the basin of the caldera.

Turn to page 113.

Luke is already shoveling out more dirt. A moment later you can see the rusty surface of a metal box.

"We found it!" Liz exclaims.

You help dig deeper, then all three of you pry the box out and haul it up to the surface.

"It's heavy," Luke says. "That's a good sign." He's panting from exertion.

"There's no lock on it," Liz points out. She works her shovel under the lid and pries it open. The lid flies back. Then you feel like shouting, but you're speechless. The box is filled with gold coins!

Turn to page 24.

20

When you reach the bottom, you stare at the remains of the wreck. Ghostly timbers, draped with seaweed and shells, loom out of the deep. Only half of the hull is visible. The rest is sunk in the sand.

A school of yellow and silver striped fish swims past. A grouper slides alongside you, its large mouth moving as if taking in great gulps of water.

The side of the ship is split in two. You swim through the opening. Hundreds of fish scatter before you.

You see the shadowy form of another diver at the far end of the hull. A long pike swims in front of your nose, then a flat purple fish with whiskers like a cat's. As you swim inside the ship, you see the remains of a table sticking out of the sand, then what looks like part of a human skeleton. It gives you an eerie feeling.

Swimming on, you notice part of a deck sticking at a narrow angle out of the sand. The wood is perfectly smooth, with no marine growths on it at all. How could that be?

You run your hand along it. The answer comes to you. This part of the ship must have been buried in the sand, perhaps for centuries, until the recent storm shifted the wreck and wrenched it free.

Turn to page 84.

You nod and reach into your pocket to touch the lucky crystal.

"Okay," Merv says. "Quiet in the audience, please." He clears his throat and reads from the piece of paper in his hand. "The equator cuts through all but one of the following countries: Brazil, Kenya, and India. Is this statement true? Or false?"

The timer begins ticking away the seconds as you try to decide how to answer. You'd like to go for the Surprise Prize—you've watched the show often enough to know that it's sure to be worth a lot more than $5,300. But if you guess wrong, you'll lose everything. Time is running out—you have to make up your mind.

If you say "true," turn to page 40.

If you say "false," turn to page 31.

If you say, "I don't know," turn to page 58.

As soon as summer vacation begins the following June, you, Luke, and Liz embark on a flight to Nairobi, the capital of Kenya. As you come through customs at the airport, a tall black man with a broad smile comes up to you.

"*Jambo!*" he says.

"Excuse me?" you say. "I don't understand."

"*Jambo* means 'hello' in Swahili, our language here," he says, his smile growing even broader. "I'm Kwame Nelson from Safari Tours. You're the contest winner, right?"

Turn to page 36.

Some people might argue about how to divide up the coins, but Mr. Johnstone and Mr. Walecka are so fair-minded that everyone is happy with their proposal. Mr. Johnstone will keep a quarter of the coins because they were found on his property. Mr. Walecka will keep another quarter because he gave you the map that you used to find the treasure. You, Luke, and Liz will share the other half of the coins.

When you get home, you find that your share alone is worth a small fortune. You sell them and put the money in the bank along with the amount you've saved already.

From then on you always keep the book *How to Get Lucky* right by your bed.

The End

You shrug. "I'm waiting for more good things to happen."

"Don't just wait," Louis says. "Make them happen!"

"What do you mean?"

"You and I could go out to the racetrack and bet on the horses. You're too young to bet, but I could buy the tickets. If you put in ten thousand dollars, you could walk away with a fortune!"

Making a fortune sounds great, but you're not sure about risking ten thousand dollars. That's almost half of what you've saved.

"I'd never suggest you bet so much if it weren't for that crystal," Louis says. "But it's hot. You've got to do something before it cools off."

You hesitate, but the prospect of winning big at the races is pretty hard to resist. "Okay, Louis," you say finally. "You're on."

The following Saturday, your cousin picks you up and drives you to the track. You have an old gray backpack slung over your shoulder. No one would ever guess you had ten thousand dollars in hundred-dollar bills in it. You can hardly believe it yourself.

Turn to page 57.

For the last few days of your visit at Wolf Ranch, you, your friends, and some of the other guests at the ranch go on a pack trip up into the mountains. It's a lot of fun. During the day you ride along a scenic trail. Fields of wildflowers blanket the mountains on one side and the verdant landscape of the valley stretches seventy miles on the other. At night you camp out under stars that look so close you feel as if you could reach up and touch them.

You arrive back at the ranch about sunset the night before you're scheduled to leave. When you go to bed, you happen to glance at the book *How to Get Lucky*, especially at rule number three—"Investigate."

We haven't investigated, you think as you drift off to sleep.

Turn to page 38.

A short while later you reach the bluff overlooking the plain. Everyone scrambles up on the rocks. You and your friends start snapping pictures with your new cameras. Zebras and wildebeests are gathered at the water hole below. In the distance giraffes lope across the plain. The early morning sun casts a golden light over the whole scene. You almost forget to breathe. Surely this is one of the most amazing sights in the world.

You pull out your lucky crystal and set it on a rock so the sun strikes it. It seems to radiate all the colors of the rainbow. It's hard to believe you could ever have bad luck as long as you own it.

Suddenly you hear a clicking sound from Kwame's direction. You turn and see not one but four lions peering at your group from only twenty yards away.

"Don't move," Martha whispers. You don't have to be told twice. You, Luke, and Liz freeze.

Kwame has his rifle ready, but he holds his fire. He doesn't want to kill the lions. In any case, if he shot at one of them, the others would be certain to charge. You hold your breath and hope that the lions will decide to move on.

Turn to page 50.

You decide it's too risky to try to go back for your lucky crystal. You suspect that it wouldn't be lucky enough to save you if you ran into a hungry lion. You stay close to the group and soon reach the safety of the Land Rover.

Kwame drives you along the road skirting the rim of the crater. You see many animals and birds, but nothing as exciting as the herds of animals you saw on the plain—or the four lions staring at you from twenty yards away.

The following day you and your friends visit the Olduvai Gorge and help anthropologists search for bones of hominids who lived in the region two million years ago. The day after that, you take a balloon ride over the Masai Mara Game Reserve.

At last your safari is over, and you bid Kwame and Martha good-bye. On the plane you think about how lucky you've been. You won a fantastic trip and made twenty-five thousand dollars. You won't have your crystal in the future, it's true. But maybe it won't matter. You have a feeling you've learned how to be lucky.

The End

"False," you say.

Merv shakes his head, and the audience groans. "I'm sorry, but I'm afraid the answer is true," Merv says. "The equator cuts through Brazil and Kenya, but it passes south of India. Well, it looks as if you'll be leaving empty-handed, but thanks for being on the program anyway."

"I enjoyed being here," you say as cheerfully as you can.

Someone shows you offstage, and before you know it, you're out of the studio and on your way home. As you walk down the street, you take the crystal out of your pocket and toss it high in the air. As it comes down you try to catch it, but somehow it glances off your knuckle, hits the street, and bounces onto a grate covering a drain. There's no chance to grab it before it slips through and disappears forever.

You stand over the drain for a moment, feeling unhappy about losing your lucky crystal. Then you shake your head and smile in spite of yourself. You didn't lose that much. The crystal didn't turn out to be so lucky after all.

The End

You look at the sheet, and again the name of one of the horses pops into your mind. "Allegra," you say.

He glances up at the scoreboard. "Wow! You're betting against Happy Time? The word is that he's going to be horse of the year."

"Maybe we shouldn't bet this time," you say.

"No, we gotta bet," Louis says. "With your lucky crystal working for us, we can't lose. And Allegra's at ten-to-one. That means every dollar pays back ten if she wins."

You glance down at the track. Allegra is number six. She's a nice-looking horse, but there are several others that look as good or better. Happy Time draws cheers from the stands as he prances by. He looks sleek and powerful and seems raring to go.

"Five minutes until post time," announces a voice on the loudspeaker.

"Come on," Louis says. "We've got to hurry."

You think for a moment. You're still not sure you want to risk ten thousand dollars on one horse race. But it's tempting to think that you could make one hundred thousand dollars in the next few minutes.

*If you decide to bet on Allegra,
turn to page 59.*

If you decide not to, turn to page 65.

"Very rarely," says Adam with a laugh. "Maybe some barracuda, but they're not likely to bother you."

"Well thanks, it sounds great. I'd love to come," you say.

After you hang up the phone, you pick up your crystal and stare at it. "A scuba diving trip —that's pretty good luck in itself," you say aloud. And you can't help thinking about the treasure the ship carried. Adam said that all of it had been located, but there just might be some that nobody has found yet. Maybe, if you take your crystal along, you'll be the one to find it.

Turn to page 43.

You glance out the window of the plane. A line of dark clouds is on the horizon and seems to be moving closer. The last thing you need right now is bad weather, but it looks as though that's what you're going to get.

You duck past the broken doorway and go into the cockpit. Jake looks around at you, his face twisted with pain.

"How ya doin', kid?" he gasps. "I'm real sorry I couldn't get us down safe."

"Don't be sorry," you say. "You made a great landing. I bet with most pilots we'd all be dead by now."

"Thanks for saying that," Jake says. "But we'll all be dead soon anyway if we don't do something. There's bad weather coming. No one's going to find us for days. And I don't think I can last that long out here. My chest hurts and it's getting worse."

Your mind races. Jake needs help fast. The radio is out, the weather's closing in, and you're the only one who can walk.

"I'll go for help," you say.

Jake nods. "There's a road and some farms a few miles away, down in the valley."

"No problem," you say. "I can cover a few miles downhill in less than an hour."

"Don't kid yourself," he says. "This is rough country. And if you go down into the wrong valley, you'll find nothing but deer, antelope, and maybe a bear or two."

"I'll find a road," you say.

Turn to page 99.

You introduce yourself and your friends. Then Kwame leads the way to his van, which is parked in a nearby lot. As he drives you to your hotel, he tells you a little about what to expect on the safari.

"You're lucky," he says. "We'll be visiting the Ngorongoro caldera, which is just across the border in Tanzania. The caldera is the huge crater of an extinct volcano, and it's one of the most spectacular game reserves in the world. And you're getting practically a private tour. The only other member of our group is a British conservationist named Martha Freeman."

"Do you think we'll see any lions?" Liz asks eagerly.

"I think you will," Kwame says with a laugh. "Just make sure you don't see them too close up."

Turn to page 72.

You're not going to risk your life on the slim chance of finding some treasure, crystal or no crystal. You back away from the cave and continue to explore the wreck, admiring the brilliantly colored fish all around you.

You and the others on the *Wayward Pelican* spend several more days exploring the wreck of the treasure ship and examining other reefs in the area. On the last day, as you are exploring a reef off Far Tortuga, you turn and see a hammerhead shark about twenty feet away. It's not coming directly at you, but a little to one side, as if it wants to size you up.

Instinctively you take out your lucky crystal as you head for the surface. It shines mysteriously in the shimmering sunlight coming through the water. The shark, attracted by the crystal, turns its head toward you.

If you hang onto the crystal, turn to page 62.

If you let go of it, turn to page 46.

38

At breakfast the next morning you show the map to Mr. Johnstone and ask if he has any ideas what the symbols on it stand for. He puts on his spectacles and squints at the map.

"Fe, Zn, Pb . . . these are symbols for different chemical elements," he says.

"Do you know which ones?"

"I'm afraid I don't," he says. "But check the encyclopedia in the bookcase in the den."

You, Luke, and Liz hurry to the den and locate the encyclopedia. You check the index and find an entry for Chemical Elements. Turning to the page indicated, you find something called the Periodic Table. It lists all the elements and the symbols for each one.

Turn to page 91.

40

"True," you say.

Merv throws up his hands and grins. "Correct!"

You jump up and down in excitement as the audience cheers. You can't wait to find out what you've won.

A map of the world flashes on a screen. "As you can see," Merv says, "the equator runs through two of the countries, Brazil and Kenya, but not the third. India is entirely in the Northern Hemisphere."

The spotlights flash on a curtain at the back of the stage. It slowly parts to reveal a twenty-foot-long blowup photo of an African plain, complete with herds of zebras, giraffes, and wildebeests, and a pride of lions.

Merv gestures at it. "The Surprise Prize," he exclaims. "A photo safari in Kenya for you and two of your friends, with new cameras and camcorders for you to take along, and on your return home, a United States savings bond worth twenty-five thousand dollars!"

The audience cheers again. You smile and shake hands and chat with Merv as the music plays to end the show. You hardly know what you're saying, though—you're too excited.

Go on to the next page.

On the way out of the studio you pull the crystal out of your pocket. You wonder whether you would have gotten on the show and won the prize without it. You can't help thinking now that it really *is* a lucky crystal. And you can't help wondering if more good luck will be coming your way.

Turn to page 14.

The day after spring vacation starts, you fly with Adam and his parents to Key West and then board a forty-foot schooner named the *Wayward Pelican*. The skipper, Jacques Roussel, welcomes you aboard.

"We'll be sailing about two hundred miles to the west, beyond the island of Far Tortuga," he says. "The wreck we'll be exploring is a Spanish treasure ship that foundered on a reef almost three hundred years ago."

"Could there be any treasure left?" you ask.

Jacques grins. "Everybody I take diving asks me that. And I always tell them the same thing— just enjoy the beautiful fish. Not a single coin has been found on that wreck in thirty years."

You and Adam help Jacques cast off the lines. The *Wayward Pelican* motors out of the lagoon and into the Gulf of Mexico. You help set the sails. Jacques sets course almost directly toward the setting sun and cuts the engine as the sails billow out in the following wind.

Turn to page 98.

A man standing nearby yells, "Allegra? You've got to be kidding. That nag hasn't got a chance."

The horses barely change position as they pass the half-mile pole. Happy Time still leads by a length, with Candy Cane second by a neck, then Gail's Delight third by half a length over Allegra.

As the horses round the far turn, most of the field is fading, but Happy Time is going as strong as ever and is widening his lead. At the next pole, he's ahead by two and a half lengths. Candy Cane, Gail's Delight, and Allegra are all nearly head-to-head.

As the horses thunder down the stretch, the fans are all on their feet, yelling.

You hold your breath and grasp your cousin's arm. Allegra is moving up on the outside!

Turn to page 76.

You're delirious or unconscious for some time. It's several days before you can understand what the doctor is saying to you.

"It was a miracle you pulled through," he says. "And you're lucky you didn't lose your leg."

"Thanks for saving me," you say weakly.

After the doctor leaves, you notice your lucky crystal sitting on the table next to your bed. Someone must have taken it out of your wet suit pocket and put it there.

You stare at it for a long time, trying to decide whether it's a lucky, or an unlucky, crystal.

The End

The best luck the crystal can give you now is to distract the shark long enough for you to reach the surface. You drop it, and it drifts slowly toward the bottom of the sea. The shark follows it down while you continue to ascend.

A half minute later the crew of the *Wayward Pelican* pulls you on board. You take a last look down into the water and see the shark swimming toward the surface, looking for the meal he missed.

You've lost your crystal, but you can't complain. It brought you luck when you needed it the most.

The End

When the *Wayward Pelican* gets back to port, you take the diamonds to a jeweler to be appraised. Their total value turns out to be almost sixty thousand dollars.

You keep a third, Jacques gets a third, and the other third is split equally among everyone who was on the trip. When you get back home, you add your share of the money to the bank account you set up after winning $5,300 on the quiz show.

For the next day or so you spend quite a bit of time staring at your crystal, wondering if more good luck will be coming your way.

Turn to page 92.

You can't pass up this chance to look for sunken treasure, especially since you have your lucky crystal along. Shining your light ahead of you, you begin to crawl into the dark cavelike space under the deck. You jump back as a patch of sand comes to life and a fish swims past your face, leaving a little cloud of sediment in its wake.

Chuckling silently at your own jitters, you move deeper into the compartment. Part of a wooden table sticks out of the sand ahead of you. You notice a lantern on one of the walls that must once have been shiny brass. Now it's corroded, covered with a greenish-gray film.

You turn to survey the rest of the room and see a pair of long, snakelike fish coming toward you. They're no bigger than one of your legs, but they look especially mean. You wonder if they're morays—you've heard they're the most vicious fish in the ocean. You break into a nervous sweat under your mask, and the faceplate begins to fog over.

The eels move closer, checking you out. You can't move freely, and you have no weapon— you'd be virtually helpless against them if they should attack.

Turn to page 94.

The big cats continue to stare at you. Minutes pass. You wonder how long they'll stand there. Maybe all day—they have nothing else to do. A mosquito lands on your arm, but you don't dare slap at it. Then, as if they had talked it over and reached a decision, the lions melt back into the jungle.

"Whew!" Luke says. "For a minute there, I thought we were going to be their lunch."

Everyone smiles except Kwame, who still looks worried. "Time to go," he says quietly.

The group starts back along the trail to the Land Rover. You've gone only a few dozen yards when you realize you left your lucky crystal on one of the rocks overlooking the crater floor. You want to run back and get it, but what if the lions are still hanging around nearby? You don't want to take a stupid risk. Still, you'd feel a lot safer if you had the crystal with you.

If you run back to get your crystal, turn to page 115.

If you decide to forget about it, turn to page 30.

"A crime? Me?" you exclaim. "I've never done anything wrong."

"We've found out that the manager of the traveling carnival has been fixing raffle tickets," the second officer says. "Turns out the raffle doesn't work by chance. We have evidence that you and your friends bought three of the winning tickets."

"We didn't buy them," you say. "We went to the manager's office to complain about getting ripped off at one of the booths, and he gave us the tickets to make it up to us."

The officers exchange glances. "Yeah, well, that's participating in a fraudulent scheme," the first officer says.

"What does that mean?"

"It means we're going to have to issue you a summons. Your friends will each be getting one, too. You'll all have to appear in Juvenile Court."

Turn to page 10.

You reach Luke on the phone and tell him to get Liz on the extension. They're both excited by the invitation, especially when you tell them about the buried treasure. Soon after school lets out for the summer, the three of you board a plane for Albuquerque, New Mexico, ready for your visit to Wolf Ranch.

When you arrive at the airport in Albuquerque, you are met by Mr. Johnstone's ranch foreman, Jake Bonner. Jake takes you to a six-seater plane, which will carry you directly to the ranch.

After you've been in the air for a little while, Jake's voice comes over the intercom. "I took us down low and fifty miles off course so you could get a look at this great scenery," he says. "Right now we're just a few thousand feet over the Pecos Wilderness Area in northern New Mexico."

You, Luke, and Liz press your noses against the window, trying to see as much as you can of what's below. There are great stretches of spruce and pine forests and valleys covered with wildflowers. Rocky peaks soar above them, the uppermost slopes still covered with snow.

"Wouldn't get this service on a regular airline," Luke remarks.

But you're not listening. You've just noticed a thin trail of smoke coming off one of the engines.

Turn to page 95.

54

You set out right away and soon reach the area shown on the map. You find a bunch of loose rocks about fifty feet east of Chimney Rock. You turn them over and dig underneath. After about twenty minutes of digging, you're tired and sweaty, and you haven't found a thing.

You all stop to rest. Luke and Liz stare at you. They're too polite to say it, but you know what they're thinking.

"I guess I didn't figure out the map after all," you say.

"Darn it!" Luke slams the blade of his shovel down in the hole he just dug.

"That made a funny sound," Liz cries.

"Keep digging there," you say.

Turn to page 19.

Micky is on one knee, adjusting the controls on the heater. You tap him on the shoulder. "Micky, we've got to land right away. I think Miss Johnstone is sick."

He glances over at her. "She's not sick. She has acrophobia—fear of heights. The only way to cure it is not to give in to it."

Miss Johnstone overhears him. "I don't want to be cured. I want to land!" she shrieks.

Luke and Liz crowd around Micky. "You've got to land," Liz says.

"Come on," Luke says. "There's a field right ahead."

"Okay, if that's what everybody wants." Micky turns down the burner, letting cooler gas enter the balloon. In a few moments it begins to descend.

A gust of wind hits the balloon and sets the basket swinging. Miss Johnstone lets out a cry.

"It's okay," you tell her. "He's taking us down now."

Micky tugs on one line, then another, guiding the balloon's descent.

Turn to page 112.

You've never been to a racetrack before. As you and Louis head for your seats, you look around, taking in the spirited thoroughbreds and the jockeys in their brightly colored silks. You reach your seats just as the horses reach the starting gate. The first race is about to begin.

"We can just watch and not bet for the first couple of races," Louis says. "But we have to bet on the third race. Three is my lucky number."

You watch as the last horse is loaded into the gate and the last door is slammed shut. Then, *they're off*!

The horses bolt out of the starting gate and race down the track. The fans yell and cheer. You begin to cheer, too, as a spunky little brindle horse makes its move on the outside and goes on to win.

You glance over at Louis. His nose is buried in the race program, which gives the name and history of every horse in every race being run that day.

"When's the second race?" you ask him.

"About twenty-five minutes." He hands you the program so you can read the names of the horses that will be competing. "Okay," he says, "hold your lucky crystal in your hand, and see if you can tell which horse will win. We'll test out your crystal on this race without spending any money."

Turn to page 71.

58

"I don't know," you say.

The audience groans. Merv pats you on the back, grinning as broadly as ever. "You did the smart thing by admitting you didn't know," he says. "After all, you wouldn't want to risk the five thousand, three hundred dollars you've already won!"

The audience applauds as you and Merv shake hands. The show is over.

You head home that night feeling pretty lucky, even though you didn't win the Surprise Prize. You take out your lucky crystal and toss it in the air. "Good going, crystal," you say. "What next?"

A week passes. You've practically forgotten about your crystal again when your friend Adam Barcus asks if you'd like to go on a scuba diving trip with him and his parents during spring vacation. "We'll be going on a boat from Key West, Florida," he says. "We're going to explore a sunken treasure ship."

"Treasure? Wow, maybe we'll find some."

"No chance of that," Adam says. "Divers got every scrap of it ages ago. But the wreck is still a neat place to dive. All kinds of fish hang out there."

"No sharks, I hope."

Turn to page 34.

"All right, let's do it," you say. You walk up to the betting window with Louis. You take the ten thousand dollars out of your backpack, but somehow you just can't bring yourself to turn it all over. You keep five thousand and give five thousand to your cousin. "I don't want to risk it all," you say.

"That's cool," he says. "This will still make you fifty thousand bucks." He shoves the bills under the bars in the teller's window.

"Five thousand on Allegra to win," he says.

The teller hardly even bothers to look up as he counts the money. Five thousand dollars must be just another bet to him, you think.

Louis takes the ticket the teller hands him and holds it in front of you. "This could be worth fifty grand," he says, "or it could be worth nothing. It all depends on your lucky crystal."

The two of you return to your seats and wait for the race to start. It seems like forever before the horses are in the gate.

They're off!

You jump to your feet and watch with clenched teeth and a racing heart as the horses pound down the track. Happy Time takes the lead almost immediately. Allegra settles into fourth place as the horses pass the quarter-mile pole.

You hold up your lucky crystal and shout, "C'mon Allegra. Go girl! Go! Go!"

Turn to page 44.

The attendant can see from your expression that you're not happy. "Heed my words," he says. "Either one of these prizes could change your life."

"Yeah, sure," you say disbelievingly.

"Look, my friend," he says. "If you want, you can have your money back instead." He shoves the two quarters toward you, but for some reason you don't feel like taking them.

"All right, I'll take the prize," you say. "Which one do I get?"

The man smiles. "Choose the one you want," he says. "The crystal or the book."

If you take the crystal, turn to page 7.

If you take the book, turn to page 67.

You slump down in your seat. Louis sits beside you, shaking his head. You can hardly believe that you just lost five thousand dollars.

You pull out your crystal and stare at it. It seems to be glittering less brightly, though that may be because the sun has just gone behind a cloud. You feel like tossing it away.

"Well," says Louis, "it was a close race. The lucky crystal almost came through."

"Almost isn't good enough," you say.

Louis shoves the program in front of you. "Hey, the next race goes off in a few minutes. I think we should give the crystal another chance. After all, Allegra did a whole lot better than most people expected. So, who does the lucky crystal like in the fourth race?"

You stare at your crystal, thinking.

Louis leans toward you. "Getting any messages from it?"

You give him a weak smile. "Yeah, I am. The crystal's telling me that it will keep giving me more luck, but that I've got to do more thinking for myself."

Louis has a puzzled look on his face. "Well, sure . . . but if it will keep giving you more luck, then let's bet on the next race. You could win back your five thousand dollars and more."

You shake your head. "No, that's where the thinking for myself comes in. I've decided I shouldn't risk my money betting on horses."

Turn to page 100.

The shark seems very interested in your lucky crystal, but you're not about to let go of it just when you need good luck the most. You close your fingers around it so the shark can't see it anymore and shove it back into your pocket.

The shark forgets all about the crystal just as you had hoped. Unfortunately, it has become very interested in *you*!

The hammerhead's powerful jaws close on your left leg. Your body is flipped violently. The shark lets go, turns, and comes back again—this time aiming straight for your head!

You look around frantically. Jacques, armed with a spear gun, is swimming toward you. The shark is almost on you. Jacques is barely in range, but he fires and scores a direct hit on the shark's snout. The hammerhead turns quickly and swims off.

Jacques helps you up to the surface. The other crew members pull you on board and apply pressure bandages on your wound. They stem the bleeding, but not before you've lost a lot of blood.

Half an hour later you're picked up by helicopter and taken to the Key West Hospital. The doctors there give you transfusions and sew up your wounds, which require sixty-seven stitches.

Turn to page 45.

64

A rock stops your slide. The impact knocks the wind out of you and sends a wave of pain through your body.

You lie there shaking for a moment, then force yourself to stand up. The frozen rain stings your face and hands. At least you're closer to the ledge now. You continue down the slope, being more careful than ever, and in a few minutes you reach your goal. Your heart is in your mouth as you stand there, your eyes searching for a sign of civilization in the broad valley below.

To your dismay you see nothing but trees wherever you look. There might be a cabin or a hunting lodge somewhere in the vast forest beneath you, but once you plunge into the trees you won't be able to see more than a few dozen yards ahead.

You turn and look up the slope you've just descended. The chill wind assaults you, the rain lashes your face, and your eyes water so that you can hardly see. Even so you can tell that the slope is too steep. There's no way you can turn around and go back up.

You turn away from the wind and continue down the mountain. A few minutes later you enter the trackless forest, wishing that you'd investigated before you started down the mountain.

You'll need more than good luck now. You'll need a miracle.

The End

"No, Louis," you say. "Something tells me I shouldn't gamble."

"It's not really gambling," he says. "With that lucky crystal it's a sure thing."

"Anyway, I'm not betting."

Louis sits glumly through the race, but you enjoy watching the horses run. Allegra, the horse you were going to bet on, comes on strong near the end and crosses the line nose-to-nose with Happy Time, the favorite. A sign comes up on the board: PHOTO FINISH.

"Just wach," Louis says. "Allegra will be the winner, and you'll have missed out on making a hundred thousand dollars!"

You have a terrible feeling he's right. But then the results come up on the board showing that Happy Time came in first and Allegra second.

Louis frowns. "Looks like we've been wasting our time out here."

"Not me," you say. "I've had a great time watching the races, and my crystal's been as lucky as ever."

"Lucky as ever? What do you mean?"

"It told me not to gamble away my money."

"You call that luck?"

"I call it good sense," you say. "And that's the luckiest thing you can have."

The End

You choose the book, and the man hands it to you. It has thick covers, and when you open it up you find only one page with just a few words on it.

Luke and Liz lean over your shoulders, and the three of you read:

Be kind.
Be honest.
Investigate.

Luke grabs the book out of your hand. "That's it? That's supposed to be a book?"

"This is ridiculous," Liz says. "I'd demand a refund."

Turn to page 11.

"Well, actually the wind does most of our steering for us," Micky says. "If it changes direction, we'll have to land somewhere else. But I think it will hold pretty much as it is today. And I can do a little steering by playing with the ropes leading up to the rim."

As Micky has been talking, the balloon has continued to expand. Soon it's fully inflated.

"This all sounds very exciting," says Miss Johnstone. "But I'm getting a little nervous. I'm not sure I ought to go."

"You'll be all right," Micky says. "This is probably safer than driving your car." He leans over the edge of the basket. "Okay, fellas, cast off," he calls to the men tending the ropes.

Miss Johnstone gasps as the balloon rises suddenly, sailing fifty feet off the ground before the wind begins to move it over the pasture.

Micky turns the burner down a little. "We don't want to rise too high," he says. "I like to keep low—you can see more that way."

You and your friends peer down over the rim of the basket at the treetops below you. You pass over a stream, then some houses, a clearing filled with wrecked cars, and a farm.

Turn to page 17.

The manager takes the book and looks at it. "This certainly is a book," he says. "In fact you're already following the advice in it. How can you complain?"

Luke frowns. "What do you mean?"

The manager runs a stubby finger down the book's single page. "See here? It says 'Investigate.' That's just what you're doing, right?" He laughs, exposing a mouthful of gold-capped teeth. "Now get out of here and enjoy the carnival, or I'll call the police."

"Go ahead," Liz says. "I bet they'd take our side."

The manager glares at her for a moment. Then he appears to relent. In a softer voice he says, "Okay, okay. I gotta give you kids credit. You're very persistent. Look, I'll make it up to you."

"How?" you all say in unison.

"Did you buy a chance on the hot-air balloon ride?"

"Yes," you say. "We all did."

"Well, I could fix it so you'll win—all three of you. Would that satisfy you?"

You glance at your friends. They both shrug, leaving the decision up to you.

If you accept the manager's deal, turn to page 86.

If you decide against it, turn to page 74.

"Miss Johnstone will be okay. And I don't want to miss seeing the town," you whisper to Luke and Liz.

"Look at that!" Luke cries suddenly, pointing to the ground.

You peer over the side and see six deer standing in a clearing in the woods. They're alert, as if sensing danger. The balloon's shadow passes over one of them, and it lopes off into the woods. The others follow, their white tails raised behind them.

Then you look down at Miss Johnstone. She is still crouched in the bottom of the gondola. You start to feel a little worried about her—she doesn't look good.

Micky notices your concerned expression. "It's acrophobia—fear of heights," he says to you in a low voice. "Best cure is to stick it out. If you give in to it, you'll never get over it."

Suddenly you feel a jolt, and the basket swings to one side. Miss Johnstone screams.

"It's all right, folks," Micky says loudly. "Just a wind shift. Nothing we can't handle."

You're not so sure. The wind has not only changed direction, but it's blowing harder. The balloon is drifting rapidly to the south. In a few minutes it crosses some railroad tracks, then it's over more woods.

Turn to page 88.

You shut your eyes, clutch the crystal, and concentrate. The name of one of the horses pops into your mind. "I think Clementine is going to win," you say.

Louis consults the program. "Clementine? Are you sure? She's a twenty-to-one shot."

"What does that mean?"

"That means people think there's only about a one-in-twenty chance she can win. Maybe you should pick another horse."

You close your eyes and concentrate some more.

"No, Clementine is it," you say.

A few minutes later the horses come onto the track for the second race. There are eight in the field. Clementine has drawn the outside post position.

Clementine is a handsome chestnut filly, but she doesn't look particularly fast. In fact she seems to be half asleep as her jockey guides her into the starting gate. You begin to think that your hunch must have been wrong.

The back gates close, then the front ones burst open. *They're off!*

The horses thunder down the track. As they round the first turn, it's Palindrome first by a length and Caper second, leading Bright Star by half a length.

A lot of people are cheering, but you and Louis are silent. Clementine is bringing up the rear.

Turn to page 6.

The next day you, Luke, Liz, Kwame, and Martha Freeman pack your gear into a Land Rover and set out for the caldera. It's a hundred-mile drive over winding dusty roads to Arusha, the town closest to the reserve. You're about halfway there when an astonishing sight comes into view—a tremendous mountain that seems to be floating in the sky.

"Kilimanjaro," Kwame says. "Highest in Africa."

"It must be a mirage," Luke says. "It looks as if it's not even connected to the ground."

Turn to page 18.

"That wouldn't be fair to the people who bought raffle tickets," you say. You glance at your friends, who nod in agreement.

"Hey, what is this, Sunday School?" the manager sneers. "You heard my offer—take it or leave it."

"We're leaving it," you say firmly.

"Come on, let's get going," Liz says. "This guy is hopeless."

The manager's face reddens. "You're the ones who are hopeless. Now get out of here!"

The three of you hurry out of the trailer. A moment later a gong sounds and an announcement comes over the speaker—"THE CARNIVAL WILL CLOSE IN FIVE MINUTES." You head for the exit.

You and the Stedmans live in different directions, so when you reach the street, you say, "See you guys in school."

"Hope your book brings you good luck," Liz says.

You smile. "Maybe we'll get a call saying our tickets won the hot-air balloon ride."

Luke laughs. "Fat chance," he says. "See ya."

No one calls to say you won the balloon ride, but about four days later, you notice a big headline in your local newspaper. It reads, CARNIVAL OWNER ACCUSED OF CHEATING ON RAFFLE TICKETS. POLICE SAY HE SOLD WINNING TICKETS TO FRIENDS.

Turn to page 104.

The wind stiffens. You pull up the collar of your parka. You figure you must be about ten thousand feet above sea level. Even though it's June, it's barely above freezing on this exposed spot.

The wall of clouds has moved closer. You look up the line of the ridge to a peak that rises several hundred feet above you. It would be a steep climb, but you think you could reach the summit in about half an hour. From there, you would be able to see a lot more of the valleys below. That would give you a better idea of which way to go.

But the clouds are moving in fast. In a little while all you'll be able to see from up there is fog. Maybe you should just pick one of the valleys and hope you'll be lucky.

If you choose one of the valleys, and start down immediately, turn to page 101.

If you climb to the summit to get a better view, turn to page 105.

With half a furlong to go, Happy Time's jockey is giving him the whip. Allegra is driving hard on the outside—she's still behind by a neck but gaining ground with every stride.

The crowd is screaming. The horses sweep under the wire. Happy Time and Allegra are nose-to-nose.

The words PHOTO FINISH light up on the scoreboard. You and Louis look at each other. There's nothing to do but wait to find out who the winner is.

A few minutes later the official results flash on the board:

1. Happy Time
2. Allegra
3. Gail's Delight

Turn to page 61.

"You're kidding," you say. "I never would have guessed we were being recorded."

"Well, you were, along with a lot of other people. And you and your friends were the only ones who weren't willing to go along with the manager's scheme."

"I'm sure glad we didn't," you say, "even if we missed out on the hot-air balloon ride."

"You didn't miss out," she says. "The man who runs the balloon ride business was so impressed with your honesty that he's offered you all a free ride. Just show up at Bennett's Farm next Saturday if you want to go."

"This is great. I've got to call Luke and Liz and tell them the news."

"Okay, I won't keep you," she says. "I hope you have a great time."

Turn to page 9.

When you wake up the next morning, the first thing you notice is the crystal sitting on your desk, glittering in the sunlight coming through the window. When you get up and walk past it toward the door, the crystal seems to take on a rosy glow. You stop and walk back the other way. The crystal definitely changes color depending on the angle you're looking at it from. Maybe it's worth fifty cents after all, you think.

During the next few weeks you almost forget about the crystal. But it comes to your mind again when your mother greets you with some exciting news one day when you get home from school.

"Guess what? Someone called from that TV quiz show called *True? Or False?* Their computer selected your name, and they want to know if you want to be on the show."

You can hardly believe it. They give away fantastic prizes on that show—you could win a lot of money. On the other hand, the questions they ask can be awfully tough. You know you'd have to be pretty lucky to get all of them right.

Suddenly you gasp. *Lucky!* That's the answer —your lucky crystal must be working. That's why you were asked to be on the show, you figure. And with luck like that going for you, how can you lose? Still, you decide to do a little studying before you go on, just to be sure.

Turn to page 12.

Micky points to the heater in the middle of the basket. "This little stove takes in ordinary air and heats it," he tells you. "As it's heated, the air rises up into the balloon, keeping it inflated."

You hear the muted roar of the flame as he turns up the burners on the stove. "Now I'm heating up the air even more," he says. "In a couple of minutes it will be hot enough to take us up. Then my assistants will let go of the ropes and we'll be on our way."

"Where are we going?" you ask.

Micky flashes you a grin. "We're in luck. There's a gentle east wind that will take us right over town. You'll be able to see your houses and maybe some of your friends waving up at you. If our luck holds, you'll be able to look straight down at the falcon's nest on the steeple of the Presbyterian church."

"Cool," you say. "Where will we land?"

"A couple of miles west of town, on the grass airstrip alongside the Connors' place. One of my assistants will be there in a van to help us fold up the balloon and bring us all back here."

"How do you steer this thing, anyway?" Liz asks.

Turn to page 68.

There is an aluminum trailer near the carnival entrance with a sign on it that says MANAGER. You, Luke, and Liz head for it.

The door is half open, and you walk inside. The place is littered with stacks of boxes and assorted equipment. There's just enough space among all the junk for a scratched and dirty Formica-topped table that serves as a desk. Papers are stacked high all over the table, leaving barely enough room for an early model computer and a telephone. Behind the table, tilting back in his chair, is an overweight, puffy-eyed man smoking a smelly cigar.

He waves you away. "Get out of here, kids. This is private."

"We have a complaint," you say.

He half-rises. "I said beat it."

"We won't beat it," Liz says. "If you won't listen to us, we'll go to the police."

The man jams his cigar butt down in an ashtray half filled with ashes and paper clips. "All right, but make it quick."

You open the book and shove it in front of him. "I paid fifty cents for a chance to win a prize, and this is what I got. It's supposed to be a book about getting lucky, but it's hardly a book at all, and there's nothing in it about luck."

Turn to page 69.

You sleep well that night, dreaming of buried treasure. The next morning at breakfast Mr. Walecka spreads an old, crinkled map in front of you.

"Since you're going to Wolf Ranch, I thought you might be interested in this map I found in the attic when I bought this place. It claims to show where treasure is buried."

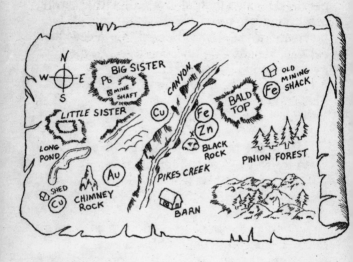

You look at the map. "I see where it mentions treasure," you say, "but I can't make much sense of it."

Go on to the next page.

"Neither can I," he says with a grin. "Otherwise I would have gone and dug it up myself. Anyway, you can take the map if you want— maybe you'll be the lucky one who can figure it out and find the treasure."

"Thanks," you say. You fold the map carefully and put it in your pocket.

A horn sounds outside. You look out the window and see a pickup truck with the words WOLF RANCH on it.

"There's my ride," you say. You thank Mr. and Mrs. Walecka and hurry out to the truck.

Turn to page 109.

You see that there is a space under the deck, like a low cave. You can't tell how deep it is or what might be under it, but you suspect that no divers have been there before. You might be the first to explore this part of the wreck. You wonder if there could be more treasure there.

You shine your flashlight under the deck, but the light doesn't carry very far. If you want to investigate it, you'll have to crawl under there.

You still have about ten minutes worth of oxygen left, but you don't like the idea of crawling along on the sand in the dark with almost no clearance over your head. If you got stuck, you'd be in serious trouble. Still, you have your lucky crystal with you. Maybe it will lead you to sunken treasure!

If you decide to explore the space under the deck, turn to page 49.

If you decide not to risk it, turn to page 37.

Micky turns away. You glance ahead and see the top of the church steeple and the gold-painted dome of the courthouse. Miss Johnstone is sobbing softly.

Luke and Liz catch your eye. "Do you think we should tell him to land?" Liz asks quietly.

If you tell Micky to land right away, turn to page 55.

If not, turn to page 70.

86

"Okay, we'll take it," you say. "When do we get to go?"

"A week from Saturday," the manager says. He strips three tickets off a roll and writes the numbers down in a notebook. Then he hands them to you. "The balloon will take off from Bennett's Farm. Be there at nine a.m. If the weather's bad, they'll give you a rain check."

A couple of days later you're at home alone when the doorbell rings. Opening it, you see two police officers standing outside. "Hello. Can I help you?" you say.

They ask for your name, and when you tell them, one of the officers says, "You don't have to answer any more questions right now if you don't want to. You may be charged with a crime."

Turn to page 51.

"Okay, everyone," Micky says. "We'll be setting down when we get past these woods. Try not to move around if you can help it. We have to keep this thing as steady as possible."

You crouch down next to Miss Johnstone. She's still sobbing softly, her eyes shut tight.

Micky adjusts the controls on the burner and tugs a bit on one of the ropes. A gust of wind jolts the balloon to one side.

There's nothing but woods visible below. The balloon is being carried farther and farther from the town. You're starting to get scared yourself.

"There's a farm ahead," Liz says, pointing.

Another gust of wind strikes. The basket swings wildly again.

"We can land there," Micky says. He turns a valve, cutting down the supply of hot air. The balloon begins to lose altitude.

You clear the treetops at the edge of the woods by about fifty feet, then drift across a cornfield, sinking lower and lower.

"Hold on," Micky cries.

The basket brushes the tops of the stalks, lifts up a few feet for a second, then comes down hard onto the ground.

Micky lets the air out of the bag. It collapses slowly, spreading over the cornstalks like an enormous blanket.

"Are you all right, Miss Johnstone?" Micky asks.

Turn to page 106.

Back in your room, you notice the book *How to Get Lucky* lying on your desk. You pick it up and throw it across the room. It lands right in the wastebasket.

Well, that certainly was a lucky shot, you think. Maybe that book has some luck left in it after all.

You retrieve the book from the wastebasket and put it back on your desk. Then you take a long, hot shower, all the while thinking about how to be lucky.

The End

The following Monday afternoon, you've just gotten home from school when your mother calls you to the phone.

"This is Miss Johnstone from the balloon ride," says the voice on the other end of the line.

"Oh, hi. How are you feeling?"

"I've never felt better, thank you. But I'm not calling about that. I'm calling to let you know how much I appreciate your having asked that man to land the balloon. I'd like to reward you and your friends somehow."

"Hey, thanks," you say.

"Not with money—I don't like that sort of thing," she says. "But I've been talking to my brother, George Johnstone. He and his wife have a wonderful place in New Mexico called Wolf Ranch. He wondered if you and your two friends would like to visit during your next school vacation. You'd be flown there in a private plane, and while you're there, you could ride horses, fish, swim, take pack trips, and have all kinds of fun. There's even a legend that Spanish explorers buried treasure near the ranch. No one's found it yet, but you kids might be the ones to do it. In any case, I think you'd have a marvelous time."

"Wow, Miss Johnstone, that sounds great," you say. "Let me call my friends and see if they can go."

Turn to page 52.

You write down the symbols on the map and then mark what each one is. Your list looks like this:

Fe: Iron
Zn: Zinc
Pb: Lead
Cu: Copper
Au: Gold

"Gold. What more could we want?" Liz exclaims.

You nod. "This map must show where gold is."

"This is cool," Luke says.

"It looks like it's buried just east of Chimney Rock," Liz says. "Come on, our flight doesn't leave until ten o'clock tonight. Let's get some shovels and start digging."

Turn to page 54.

92

A couple of weeks later your cousin Louis, who has just graduated from college, drops by your house to say hello. His eyes light up when he hears about your lucky crystal and the money you've made.

You show him the crystal. He holds it up to the light. "Wow, it's so bright—as if there's some power source in it," he exclaims.

"There's power in what happens with it," you say.

"I believe it," Louis says. "You've made a lot of money with this crystal, and I bet you could make a lot more." He holds it up and waves it in the air. The crystal changes color as he moves it around.

Turn to page 26.

The morays circle you and then swim off. You check your watch and see that you have only five minutes worth of air left. It's probably going to take longer to get out of this space than it did to get into it. If you go much further, you'll be taking a big risk.

As you shine your light around one more time, it falls on an object you hadn't noticed before—a chest half buried in the sand. You swim over to it. There's an ancient lock on it that's mostly rusted away. You tug at the lock, and it falls off. You try to lift the lid, but it's stuck. You wedge your knife under the lid and try to pry it open. Still stuck. You work the knife around the edges of the lid, trying to open it again every few inches. Suddenly the lid gives way. With a great heave, you lift it off.

The chest is almost empty, but there are dozens of glittering stones at the bottom.

Diamonds! And they're big ones—they must be worth a fortune!

You scoop up the diamonds and put them in your collecting pouch. Then you carefully work your way out of the cave. You reach the surface just as your air is running out. Your lucky crystal has come through again!

Turn to page 47.

Jake's voice comes over the intercom again, but this time he sounds worried. "Buckle up, kids. We've got a little emergency."

The jet goes into a dive. The lights suddenly blink off. The smoke gets thicker, and you can see flashes of red flame on the wing.

You glance at Luke and Liz. Their mouths are taut, their eyes wide. They look as scared as you feel. You grip the armrests tightly. The plane swerves dizzily, then banks. The mountains seem to be rushing up at you as the plane hurtles toward the ground.

You grab your jacket from the seat next to you and hold it against your chest for added padding, though you know it won't help much if the plane hits hard.

The right wing dips almost ninety degrees, then levels. The nose of the plane pulls up, and your body is wrenched violently to one side. The remaining engine roars, then there is a terrific jolt and the noise of ripping metal as the plane grazes the ground. It bounces and then hits again with a sickening crunch. Your upper body is thrown forward. Your head strikes the seat in front of you with a thud.

The plane has touched down on an icy mountain slope. It skids along for a few terrifying seconds. Suddenly it noses down into a shallow gully and comes to an abrupt stop. Your head slams into the seat again. You feel waves of pain. Then you black out.

Turn to page 102.

You pick your way down the steep incline, heading for the valley where you saw the smoke. The rain is falling harder now, and the wind threatens to throw you off-balance at every step. You can't see more than a few hundred yards ahead of you. But the weather is at your back. You're sure you can make it now that you have a goal.

Two hours later, soaked, bruised, cut, and aching, you stumble down a wooded slope into a cow pasture. There is a barn only fifty yards away and a farmhouse beyond it. A farmer comes out of the barn and starts toward the house. You yell and run over to him. You introduce yourself and explain what happened.

"Well, come on inside and get yourself cleaned up while I call the authorities," the farmer says. You follow him into a large kitchen lit by a roaring fire. A plump, smiling woman is sitting at the table. She rises to greet you.

"By the way, I'm Ben Walecka," the farmer says. "This is my wife, Peggy."

Turn to page 108.

That evening, the gentle motion of the boat rocks you to sleep. You're awakened by the early morning sunshine. It's a beautiful sailing day. You spend part of it steering, part of it dozing in the hammock on the foredeck, and part of it taking scuba lessons from the crew.

About noon the following day, the *Wayward Pelican* reaches the buoy that marks the location of the wreck. After dropping anchor, the crew members help you and the Barcuses on with your scuba gear.

"This should be an interesting dive," Jacques says. "There's been a terrific storm since the last time I was out here. I heard the waves were so strong they shifted the wreck and broke off part of it."

"We'll soon see how it looks," says Mr. Barcus as he zips up his wet suit and straps on his scuba tank.

When everyone is ready, you slip over the side one by one and begin the forty-foot descent.

Turn to page 20.

Jake half-smiles. "I have to hand it to you, you're a gutsy kid. Well, you'd better get going. It won't be long until we get a real hard rain, or maybe snow."

"I'll be as fast as I can," you say.

"Don't forget to keep track of which way you go so you can tell people where we are," Jake says.

"Okay."

The plane door has been completely ripped off. You stand in the opening for a moment and then hop down, landing in about four inches of soft, granular snow.

You're above the timberline, so you can see a good distance. About a quarter of a mile away, a steep ridge runs like a spine up and down the mountain. You set out for it, hoping to get a better view from there.

You reach the ridge after about a twenty-minute hike through the snow. From this vantage point, you can see steep slopes on either side leading down into separate valleys. The view of each valley is blocked by rock ledges about a thousand feet below. The ridge you're on, which serves as the barrier between the two valleys, rises steeply farther down the mountain. There's no way you'd be able to cross from one valley to the other down there.

If Jake is right, there are some farms in one of these valleys. But which one?

Turn to page 75.

Louis looks crestfallen. "Okay," he says. "But I think you're missing a great opportunity."

When you get home, you set your crystal on your desk. It makes a nice decoration. And after thinking about your experiences with it, you decide that it's given you the best luck of all—it's taught you to think for yourself.

The End

You don't want to waste time and energy climbing the peak if you won't be able to see anything anyway. So you look down the mountain, wondering which route is more likely to lead to civilization. A harsh wind is blowing across the top of the ridge. The valley to the right, which faces south, will be more sheltered, and you figure that's as good a reason as any for heading into it.

Suddenly the wall of clouds blots out the sun. The mountains, which looked so beautiful from the plane, suddenly seem dark and foreboding. You tighten the straps on your backpack and scramble down the south side of the ridge, picking your way among the rocks and hillocks, trying to move quickly without stumbling. You reach a ledge. The slope beneath it is so steep you have to face it, as if you were climbing down a ladder, and use your hands as well as your feet to keep from falling.

Turn to page 110.

You regain consciousness a few minutes later. Liz is bending over you. Her forehead is caked with blood and an ugly purple bruise is forming on her cheek. Luke is stretched out across two seats. His head is propped up by his jacket and his eyes are open, but he looks pale, and there is a painful-looking lump on his temple.

"How are you?" Liz asks.

You unbuckle your seat belt and wiggle your arms and legs. "Well, I've got a real bummer of a headache, but other than that I think I'm okay." You stand up. "How about you, Luke?"

He manages a weak smile. "Okay, except I feel kind of dizzy."

"He may have a concussion," Liz says.

You notice the cockpit door is broken off. "How's Jake?" you ask Liz.

"He's got some cuts and bruises. They don't look too bad. But he says he's got a bad pain in his chest. He's afraid it's his heart."

Turn to page 15.

Serves him right, you think. He had it coming to him.

You read the rest of the story and find that the police had a court order to plant a bug in the manager's office. They recorded conversations in which he revealed that instead of running the lottery legitimately, he sold the winning tickets or gave them away to his friends.

You've hardly finished reading the article when the phone rings. It's Luke and Liz, calling to ask you if you've seen the story.

"I sure have. It will be interesting to see what happens," you say.

What happens is very surprising. The following week you get a call from the assistant district attorney, Ms. Roraback. She tells you she's the prosecutor on the lottery ticket case.

"What can I do for you?" you ask. You wonder if she's going to ask you to testify.

"You don't have to do anything," she says. "The manager already confessed. I'm just calling to give you some news."

"What kind of news?"

"One of the conversations the police recorded was of the manager offering you winning tickets to shut you up about the phony prize you got at the ball-toss booth."

Turn to page 78.

You remember that the book *How to Get Lucky* said to "Investigate." You start climbing up toward the summit, watching anxiously as the oncoming wall of clouds blots out the sun.

You make good progress at first, but after a few minutes the strength seems to be ebbing from your body. You have to rest every few steps. You're not used to this altitude, and your pack begins to feel as heavy as if it were loaded with bricks.

With each step you take, the air becomes a little thinner and the wind a little fiercer. The slope steepens as you get closer to your goal. For the last few yards you have to hug the ground and claw your way up, digging your feet into the crusty snow. Finally, on your hands and knees, you reach the summit.

The cold wind is blowing so hard by this time that you can hardly stand up. But it's still clear enough to see into the valleys. Looking down, you can see that the valley on the right is an unbroken expanse of spruce and pine. The one on the left is more open. You can see a high stretch of meadowland, then mixed forest and fields lower down, and lower still, a wisp of smoke rising from the valley floor.

You feel like cheering despite your weariness. Smoke means people and civilization!

A moment later a gust of wind almost blows you off the summit. You're glad to leave it.

Turn to page 97.

106

Instead of answering, she stands up, grips the rim of the basket, and stares out over the cornfield. Fortunately, she seems uninjured, and the color is coming back to her cheeks. In fact her face has grown red with anger. She turns to Micky. "This is certainly *not* what you advertised, young man!"

Micky says, "I'm sorry, Miss Johnstone. We can't control the weather, you know."

"You could have controlled yourself," she replies. "Instead of being so heartless and refusing to land when I was suffering so."

At that moment it begins to rain—hard.

"I'll get help," Micky says. He vaults over the rim of the basket and heads toward the farmhouse, which is about a quarter of a mile away.

The rest of you do your best to stay dry as you sit and wait. Miss Johnstone is in no condition to wade through a cornfield, and you don't feel right about leaving her. You know what she's thinking—if you'd asked Micky to set the balloon down when she wanted him to, you'd all be on your way home by now.

As it is, it's about three hours before you walk in your door, wet, chilled, and not very happy. And to top it off, your bike is still stuck out in the rain at Bennett's Farm.

Turn to page 89.

108

Mrs. Walecka invites you to sit in front of the fire and warm up. She hurries off to find you some dry clothes while Mr. Walecka picks up the phone and calls the police.

"They'll have a helicopter up there before dark," he says when he hangs up.

You call your family and the Stedmans to tell them what happened—and that Luke and Liz will be okay.

A couple of hours later word comes that a rescue helicopter has found the wrecked plane and taken Jake, Luke, and Liz to the nearest hospital. You call the hospital and get through to Luke.

"How's everyone doing?" you ask.

"Good. Liz and I will be out of here tomorrow morning. Jake will be in a while longer, but they say he's going to be okay, thanks to you."

"That's great news."

"Oh, did you hear from Mr. Johnstone?"

"No."

"He's sending someone to pick us up and take us to Wolf Ranch tomorrow," he says. "So we'll still have our chance to look for that buried treasure."

"Great. See you then."

Turn to page 82.

Wolf Ranch is nestled on the western slope of San Pedro Mountain, about fifty miles from where your plane went down. The owners, Mr. and Mrs. Johnstone, couldn't be kinder. They invite you to ride, swim, and fish to your heart's content.

But you and your friends have something else on your mind—trying to figure out the map Mr. Walecka gave you. Unfortunately, Luke and Liz can't tell anything more from the map than you can.

"What do you think it all means?" Luke asks.

"I don't know," Liz says, "but all these funny symbols look like they could be a code or something."

"If it's a code, I sure can't see how to crack it," Luke says.

"Me neither," you say. "Now I know why Mr. Walecka said he couldn't make sense of it."

"Well, no sense wasting our whole vacation trying to figure it out," Liz says. "Let's go riding."

You put the map away and saddle up along with Luke and Liz, but you don't enjoy the ride as much as you should. You're feeling a little dejected because you haven't been able to decipher the treasure map.

Turn to page 27.

Farther down, the slope is less steep, but the ground is covered with shards of rock and shale. You're wearing comfortable running shoes, but what you really need are hiking boots. A broken leg or even a sprained ankle here could mean death.

The sky is almost black now, and a mixture of rain and snow is flying in the wind. You've got to keep moving.

It's only a few hundred feet more now to the ledge that's blocking your view of the lower valley. But this last stretch is very steep. You pick your way carefully, holding out your arms to keep your balance.

Suddenly you lose your footing and fall. Sliding down the steep grade, you twist and turn, trying to grab hold of something.

Turn to page 64.

A few minutes later the basket brushes the ground. It bounces back up a few feet into the air and comes down again with a thud. The balloon collapses and flops onto the tall grass.

Miss Johnstone gives a little gasp. Then a thin smile forms on her pale, wrinkled face. "Oh," she says. "It's so good to be on the ground."

"Glad you feel better," Micky says. "Now I'll have to find a place where I can call and get someone to pick us up." He hops over the rim of the gondola and walks toward a white farmhouse on the other side of the field.

A chill wind comes up, causing the balloon bag to flutter and flap on the grass. But the basket stays firmly on the ground.

Miss Johnstone has taken a comb and mirror from her purse. She wipes her eyes with a tissue, combs her hair, and dabs a bit of powder on her nose.

The wind grows stronger, and you feel a few drops of rain hit your arms.

"Do you feel up to walking to the farmhouse, Miss Johnstone?" you ask. "I think you'd be more comfortable waiting there than out here."

"Yes, thank you," she says.

You and your friends help her climb over the rim of the basket, and you all slog across the field to the house. Soon you're sitting around a table in the farmer's kitchen, sipping hot chocolate and basking in the heat from a woodburning stove.

Turn to page 90.

You estimate that the walls on the opposite side of the crater must be six or eight miles away. There is a lake in the valley that looks smoky blue from this distance. You see a herd of zebras drifting toward the lake. The zebras at the edges of the herd stop frequently to sniff the air. They must be wondering, as you are, whether lions are watching them through the tall grass.

"Come on," Kwame says. "We'll follow this trail down toward the plain. Stay close together and be very quiet. I'll take you to a rocky bluff overlooking a water hole. We'll have a good view of the animals from there."

You follow Kwame down a trail bordered on either side by heavy brush. You don't have to ask why you're all supposed to stay together— Kwame is the only one carrying a rifle.

Turn to page 29.

You break away from the group and run back toward the rock. You hear a shrill whistle from Kwame calling you back, but you don't even look around. You're sure that once you reach the crystal, you'll be safe. The rock where you left it is just around the next turn in the trail.

Also just around the turn is an old leopard. It's too slow to catch zebras on the plain below—but not too slow to catch you!

Your last sight is of your lucky crystal, glittering on the rock just a few feet farther down the trail.

The End

ABOUT THE AUTHOR

EDWARD PACKARD is a graduate of Princeton University and Columbia Law School. He developed the unique storytelling approach used in the Choose Your Own Adventure series while thinking up stories for his children, Caroline, Andrea, and Wells.

ABOUT THE ILLUSTRATOR

TOM LA PADULA graduated from Parsons School of Design with a B.F.A. and earned his M.F.A. from Syracuse University. For over a decade he has illustrated for national and international magazines, advertising agencies, and publishing houses. Mr. La Padula is on the faculty of Pratt Institute, where he teaches a class in illustration. During the spring of 1992 his work was exhibited in the group show "The Art of the Baseball Card" at the Baseball Hall of Fame in Cooperstown. The Johnson & Johnson corporation recently acquired one of Mr. La Padula's illustrations for their private collection. Tom La Padula resides in New Rochelle, New York, with his wife, son, and daughter.

CHOOSE YOUR OWN ADVENTURE®

A CHOOSE YOUR OWN ADVENTURE® BOOK

PASSPORT

THE NEWS TEAM THAT COVERS THE WORLD

YOU MAKE THE NEWS!

You are an anchor for the Passport news team.
Together with Jake, your cameraman, and Eddy,
an investigative journalist, you travel the world on
assignment, covering firsthand some of the hottest
events in the news.